The Manifesto on a Beautiful Society

By Tracy Agidi

Foreword

Tracy, this is a stunning collection of work that reflects a rare gift of writing. Your poetry is chokingly poignant at times, with a probing insight into the joys and tortures of the human condition. Please do show this to the Head of English(Mrs Dron) and try to get this published.   Miss Cooper, English Dept, Westcliff High School for Girls

Tracy, you possess a flair for creative writing. It is expressive, raw in places and incredibly moving. Your intelligence and curiosity about the justice of global situations underpins the content of these poems. I agree with Miss Cooper-you should seek publication-and keep writing no matter what!
Ms Dron, Head of English Dept, Westcliff High School for Girls

CONTENTS

Preface

I am not a rebellious teenager with an issue about society. I am not an adolescent with a problem with authority. And I am not an uncontrollable feminist that wants women to rule the world. To tell you the truth, I think that society is magnificent, inspiring and enchanting in a variety of ways. I am able to see the love and witness the compassion humanity bestows. I can also understand the intimacy and acknowledge the nature of human altruism and for that I am so very thankful. At the end of the day, I am lucky. Aren't I? I can talk without fear and seek comfort and lament about things that really do not have to be lamented about.

What about the things that I have a right to lament about? So I *will* lament about them but not right now. This anthology was originally a project; a display of my skill for an activity in school. But now it is so much more. Not because it impacted a substantial amount of people, because it didn't; it also didn't change the world and alter the way our complex minds think. But it changed the way I thought and for now...that is enough. Thank you for reading.

Acknowledgements

All authors that I have admired and idolised throughout my life seem to always include acknowledgement page in their works. As a child, I never truly understood the value of it, and until recently I would close the novel without reading that page. However, I now understand the value of this key section(it is a place to share your entire gratuity), because a book is like a child and a child cannot be raised without a village.

I would like to say thank you to my family. Thank you for listening to every single one of my poems, night and day. Even when I would disturb you during your own time, you listened and that encouraged me to carry on. My little sister, Daisy, you always gave me ideas when I couldn't think of any. I would especially love to say thank you to my mother for pushing me along and always providing time to listen to my work. You supported me and inspired me throughout. Thank you.

Also, I would like to say thank you to my friends. For sitting down to read my latest poems during lunch times when I knew that you probably were desperate to leave but decided to stay because that's what friends do. I would also love to say thank you for letting me do interviews on your takes of being Muslim and the Islamophobia that you encounter at times. I know that this was a hard topic to discuss and I acknowledge your bravery. Thank you.

Furthermore, I would love to say thank you to my year 9 English teacher, Ms Cooper for always

inspiring and motivating me. Without you, this book will not see the light of the day. English has become my passion and you had a part in making it that. Thank you for always giving me constructive criticism and taking time to be my assessor.
Thank you to everyone who helped me along this path.

CHAPTER 1 LOVE

1(i) Dear Daddy
When I was born,
I'm sure you smiled,
It didn't matter that I wasn't a boy,
Because I was yours,
The same way you were mine.

Do you remember?
That summer in France,
Where you held my hand so tight,
Because I was yours,
The same way you were mine.

And a few summers later,
When I twirled in my new uniform,
I recall your grin,
Because I was yours,
The same way you were mine.

Tracy Agidi

I'm sorry,
For the words I spoke,
And the screams I yelled,
And the 'I hate you' I said,
I don't blame you,
For the words you spoke,
And the screams you yelled,
But you never said I hate you,
Because I was yours,
The same way you were mine.
I never told you about that night,
And the words he said,
As I bled in tramp and drowned in whore,
Because he thought that I was his,
But he was never mine.

I lied to myself,
It was because he was your friend,
Your best friend,
And what type of daughter would I be to ruin that,
But that wasn't why.

It was because I didn't want it,
Feel it, hear it and bear it,
The disappointment and shame,
And the fact that I wasn't innocent,
That I was tainted and ruined and defiled,
No longer your innocent little girl,
So how could you be mine?

So I beg of you,
Teach my little brother,
That 'no' means 'no'
To not taint or ruin or defile,
The same way you taught me,
That I was yours,

And you were mine

1(ii) Accepting the Light

My body is untainted,
My mind is unsullied,
 My heart remains pristine,
 My soul prevails as.

The silver on my ring is a reminder of my commitment,
My devotion, my inexorable dedication,
An everlasting contract to God,
And with one glance - my temptations are swayed.

I withstand the torture,
My faith is my armour,
And I smile and laugh and proudly bear it,
My abstinence is ultimately my choice.

Yet who are you to say?
That my parents have slid this jewellery on me,
Who are you to say?
That I am a fake: that I need to *get with the time.*

And when the temptations advance,
And thoughts of kisses and caresses surface,
I remember that my body is a temple of the Holy Spirit,
And I accept the light again.

1(iii) And teach you did...
You taught me how to paint,
One beautiful stroke after another,
And paint I did,
You taught me how to sing,

Jazz blues floating around,
And sing I did,
You taught me how to drink,
Beer can in my hand,
And drink I did,
You taught me how to laugh,
Poking the dimple in my cheek,
And laugh I did.

You taught me how to kiss,
Your mouth tasting of bitter-sweet vodka,
And kiss I did,
You taught me how to touch,
With gentle caresses, you played me like a violin,
And touch we did,
You taught me to fear,
All the possibilities of the world,
And I almost drowned in fear,
You taught me to love,
As we held one another,
And I rose to the top in love.

But you also taught me to hurt,
When you stopped answering the phone,
And – by God – hurt I did,
You taught me to worry,
About colleges and futures and us,
And worry, I did,
You taught me to shout,
Because we weren't us any more,
And I shouted and shouted and shouted,
You taught me to cry,
When we went on a 'break'
And I cried because it couldn't be fixed.

But he taught me to smile,
About the little things all around me,

And smile I did,
He taught me to forgive,
To let go of the anger inside me,
So I forgave one bit at a time,
He taught me to dance,
And we danced at our wedding,
And I danced all night long,
He taught me to sleep,
As he got up for our son,
And I slept soundly.

He taught me to love,
He taught me that love still exists,
Even after I thought it never could again,
And so I will remember my first love,
That taught me to paint, sing, drink and laugh,
That taught me to kiss, touch, fear and love,
That taught me to hurt, worry, shout and cry,
And I thank you first love,
Because without you,
I never would have fallen in love with him,
My second love,
And fall I did

1(iv) All of Me
What is this that I see?
A roll of skin, as clear as can be,
What about my skin-tight jeans?
A muffin top, stretching the seams,
What about my brand new shirt?
Breasts too large, afraid it will burst,
Now let's look at my face,
Pimples that I cannot erase,

What about my perfect nose?
Too large, my eyes too close,
And let us not forget my rosy cheeks?
Far too plump, more critiques,
Now we shall travel down,
My large derriere, it is too round,
What about my feet?
Ankles are thick, practically obese,
So I grab the magazine,
Stare at the woman I shall never be,
But I still laugh and smile,
Walk out of the house with style,
Because imagine if we were all the same,
Would that not be a shame?
So maybe I'm only me,
But who would I rather be?

1(v) Unavoidable!

They are perpetually moving targets,
Fragile to disturbance or loss,
Unable to understand the difference between right and
wrong
They are lacking the attribute of invincibility
Maybe that is why they call the end unavoidable.

There is a child,
Lying on a bed, forlorn and dismal,
Her bare head is prominent in the light,
The ultimate price is approaching,
Even one as young as she, she is aware.

There is a boy,
Standing by a viaduct, broken and eternally tormented,

His hands fly towards the heavens and he leaps,
The vast lake draws closer, its turquoise hue with its cerulean shards,
It engulfs the adolescent

There is a woman,
Behind a wall, gripping a deadly weapon,
Multiple thoughts flying about her mind-
Regret, depression, candid demand
She unleashes it with tears falling down her face,
    As those fall around her in a random sequence

And there is a girl and a boy,
Gripping hands tightly as they soar across the land,
Smoke erupting from the shadows behind them,
Screams and cries cutting into them,
As they flee from a country torn apart

Who are we to say that the end is inevitable?
Unpreventable, inexorable, inescapable,
What if it was evitable?
Avertable, preventable, escapable,
Maybe the end is avoidable

CHAPTER 2: ISSUES

2(i) Message to my mum

Mum, I did it for you. I did this for everyone. Don't blame me – just remember that I did it for you. I mean…it's okay to be sad, upset and even disappointed, but that will fade and it will all feel better. Trust me –I know. Just remember that I did it for you, kay?

It's not your fault either. Yeah, you could have cried less because whenever you cried, it only convinced me that my plan was right. And I couldn't stand it when you touched my rib and you made that disturbing little whimper and all I could do was stand there, emotionless, like a living statue. Or when you placed the video camera in the room so there was nowhere – literally nowhere – I felt safe, without the pinpricks of judgement that pulsate and throb in my brain. And when I heard you weeping into your wine glass; the Chardonnay that you only take out when you are depressed and on the phone with Jane, saying, "I don't know what to do. It's not the same." But here's the truth mother: I didn't know what to do, and you are so completely utterly right – it won't be the same. It will be better – *you* will be better.

I lied. I lied so much and I didn't feel any guilt. Does that make me a bad person? I don't think so. I think it makes me a messed-up, broken person and that just confirms that what I'm doing is right. But still, I'm sorry for that. When you were at work on the weekend, I was sneaking boys into my room because for one beautiful ethereal second I felt cherished and adored and wanted. And like an addiction, I desired more and so I invited another boy in when the last left like a perpetually moving train. Yet it sort of backfired on me. The last boy was a rugby player from the seaside that had a movie-star smile and cornflower blue eyes. As I unbuckled my bra and dropped it on the newly-vacuumed carpet, I felt his stare. I turned around expecting the usual – a lustful glance with darkened sleepy eyes but instead I was greeted with a grimace. And like an idiot, I followed his line of sight and he was staring at the bones in my shoulders and wrists and knees. But that didn't stop him from pushing me on the bed and getting down to business. Too explicit, too bad! I also lied about my weight because I relished that tentative smile you gave me when – *oh goody I gained another pound!* I drank three bottles of water before you entered with the weighing scale and sewed rocks into the pocket of my skinny jeans.

I have this theory about people: throughout life, people always say that it's okay to be unique and that everyone is perfect in their own quintessential way. But, how come when I wanted to be perfect in my own quintessential way, I was labelled as a freak, an anorexic or bulimic or attention-seeker. But I wasn't that, I promise. I only wanted to be sculpted by the sculptor, painted by the painter, watched by the watcher and written by the writer. People believe in rights and confidence but the truth of the matter is – the minute you make someone uncomfortable, it's just not alright. And if you don't change then they'll make you change – with words and fists and laughter and smirks. Do you remember when I was seven? We made that scrapbook about all of the things we like; it was filled with pictures of puppies and ball gowns strewn with diamonds and rhinestones. Do you remember what you asked me that day? I never forgot. You held a strand of my black cornrow in between your manicured fingers ,gave me a grin and said, "What do you want to be when you're all grown up, baby?" Then I said, "Mamma, I'm gonna be famous!" You were probably thinking that I wanted to be an actress or singer or model but that wasn't it. To me, fame was being known and recognised, people talking about you and watching your every step and analysing you. A crowd looking at you, not because of your talent but because you were you and that was interesting. Were these thoughts a sign of what was to come? Were they a signal you should have seen? Probably, but how could you know all of this from, "Mamma, I'm gonna be famous!"

Don't go into the bathroom. Call the ambulance. And in the extremely rare case that I commit suicide, which would be so laughable, take me off life support! Do it because you love me. And whatever happens next will be better that being here. I guess living just wasn't cut out for me. Please make the funeral quiet. I love you.

2(ii) Will it ever be enough?
It started as a dare,

Trying to be tough,

And now I begin to wonder,

Will it ever be enough?

My hands shake as I hold it,

And I wince as I press it on my skin,

I sigh as I feel the temporary calmness,

And wish I never injected it in.

And she knows that something is going on,

But she would rather not say a word,

Yet in my head I beg,

'Mum, please come and help me back up!"

Tracy Agidi

It hurts,

Knowing that I have no control,

Living knowing I gave the control to a needle,

Admitting that I am living without a soul,

And one day it is just too much,

Knowing that I am ruined beyond repair,

Unable to be cured,

No longer needed, no need to be there

And I smile, smile, smile,

As I inject one, two three,

Keep pressing, not stopping,

Keep taking in, never giving out,

Keep pressing, not stopping,

Keep taking in, never givin—

2(iii) The Art of Gravity

Who doesn't have dreams?

When we are little, the universe is at our fingertips,

We have nothing holding us back,

No gravity holding us down,

But sometimes gravity is good,

Sometimes it's the only thing keeping us here,

In this messed up world,

Where good is bad and bad is good,

And it's so hard to see the truth from lies,

That eventually you decide to not see,

To not smell or feel or breathe,

So, ask me if I have any dreams?

I have one,

I dream of my self-preservation to vanish,

To be brave and just do it,

To not stop halfway spitting out pills,

To finish what I started,

But I also have another dream,

That gravity will grow stronger,

That something...anything will be enough to hold me down,

That the universe will not let me go,

And that I will be brave enough to not do it.

I will be brave enough to stay,

To make new dreams

CHAPTER 3:EQUALITY

3(i) A true feminist?

What does it say about me?

Too afraid to say the truth,

Too upset to just submit,

I remember age twelve,

Pigtails, some acne and still using a scooter,

Was about to go outside when i heard – no!

And my mama told me that my shorts were too short,

But that's what parents do right?

Protect us? Teach us?

So I changed,

Boy, do I regret that,

Because my clothing does not define me,

Telling a girl to cover up,

Is telling a girl that her body is shameful, dangerous,

Dare I say it – sickening?

But wearing jeans doesn't stop the catcalls,

And the whistles down the goddamn street,

And the sly pats that make me want to disappear.

But – now listen carefully because this is shocking,

I don't deserve to disappear.

I don't need to close my legs,

I don't need to wear long sleeves,

I don't need to be a mother,

What I do need to do is simple,

I need to walk down the street with pride,

I need to shout when i feel a sly pat,

I need to take control of my own life because...

Please remember that a woman is not your property,

That you only call me a slut because my sexuality scares you,

The manifesto on a beautiful society

Intimidates you, shakes you right to the core,

But that's not my fault at the end of the day

Please remember that a feminist is not synonymous

With man-hating witch,

But means someone who believes,

Like I do

That's a girl,

Maybe your sister, or cousin, or daughter or mother,

Shouldn't be too afraid to say the truth

Too upset to submit,

They should know what a true feminist is.

Tracy Agidi

3(ii) Girl with skin the colour of the darkest night

There is a girl,

With skin the colour of the darkest night,

And eyes like the sweetest caramel,

Her teeth are the brightest white.

The catcalls in the playground,

She turns her face away,

As they form a circle around her,

Chanting, 'This isn't your country – you can't stay!"

She creates a new world,

Of magic and lovely spells,

Where she is embraced despite her skin,

No longer imprisoned in a cell

But one day it is too much,

When they all begin to snigger,

As they touch her hair and her skin,

And they whisper in her ear, 'Go home – Nig***.'

She takes her anger,

Her fury and humiliation,

She writes and writes,

And formulates a new creation

But that was years ago,

Yet that does not make it okay,

Because I was once that girl,

And I am here to stay.

3. (iii) Stars can't shine without a bit of darkness

They say the mirror doesn't lie,

And reflections tell only facts,

But when I stare at myself,

I can't stop the way I react.

I look down,

Staring blatantly at my bareness,

Tracy Agidi

I flinch at what I see,

And almost laugh at the unfairness.

I creep out,

Leaving the leaflet on the table,

The night sky is dark and cold,

And with it I forget about the labels.

It is peaceful here,

An inky shroud,

The stars like fairy lights,

I look up at the barely-there clouds.

But for once I don't feel calm,

Even when I count my clear-glossed nails,

The terror envelops me,

And like clockwork – I am off the rails.

And I want to tear open my face,

Cut away the part that makes me think,

So slowly I close my eyes,

And into infinity, I sink

There I am me,

I place the curling-iron on my makeup pile,

And stare at my pink-bordered mirror,

And for once – I can smile.

And in this beguiling utopia,

My father calls me 'sweetheart'

My mother calls me 'her special girl'

And with a kiss I depart.

The boy next door,

With his sea-green eyes,

Is waiting in his car,

When I enter – he places his hand on my thigh.

In this Garden of Eden,

There is no Joseph Ledge,

I am known as Megan,

And I have womanly curves not male edges.

I open my eyes,

And stare up at the night sky,

I recite details of my near transition,

Sit up, stand up, and sigh.

And for once I feel so perfectly insignificant,

As I stare up at the stars glowing in the twilight,

Because I am the star, one of a million,

All of us creating a divine light

And the darkness that surrounds me is the insecurity,

And the ignorance, and the hate,

But like a star, my glow cannot be dulled,

And, no matter what, I will be great.

3(iv) Muslimah

Killer, murderer,

Gravel beneath my knees,

Slaughterer, gunman,

Blood forming between my teeth,

Suicide, death,

My hijab puts me at ease.

Fury, anger,

Alone, forsaken, I sit,

Fear, dread,

I lie that I am fine with it,

Dismay, loss,

I tighten my hijab bit by bit.

Blood, ash,

I cannot take my eyes away,

Smoke, screams,

The tears fall anyway,

Ruin, massacre

And to Allah, I pray.

Self-resentment, insecure,

I take it off, ever so slowly,

Tracy Agidi

Shock, revelation,

This is what they want, to control me?

Pride, self-assurance,

And with my hijab on, I smile boldly.

My hair is covered, my face too,

Not to plant the bombs that I know you think I do,

My beauty is hidden, my modesty is mine,

Do not make it seem as if that is a lie,

I pray to my God, devoted I remain,

ISIS and I, we are not the same,

I am sorry if you cannot see the truth,

But I will no longer take your abuse,

I brush the gravel off my knees,

Spit the blood from my teeth,

And I know that Allah can see,

How my hijab puts me at ease.

3v. Ten little fingers, ten little toes

You are a distant memory,

An image of gone with the wind dreams,

A piece of me that never left,

And it never will , it seems.

I was sixteen,

About to face the world,

When I felt a movement,

And my future unfurled.

I lied to myself, over and over again,

When I pulled my face from the toilet, I lied,

When I could not zip up my skirt, I pretended,

It was only when I saw the pink plus that I cried.

I never told anyone,

And who would suspect?

That the school president,

Was less than perfect

I played along,

Maintaining my flawless illusion,

When as a bump formed,

I felt as if I was walking towards my own execution.

And then it all changed,

When this courage outweighed my dread,

A need for confirmation,

How I wished I had stayed instead.

And you were beautiful,

In my stomach you slept,

I could count your little fingers and toes,

And in the clinic, I wept.

I could imagine a future,

Just you and I,

I stroked away a wisp of you downy hair,

Never would your wants be denied.

The manifesto on a beautiful society

May, June, July,

I dreamt of maple-wood cots

August, September, October,

And bows speckled with pink dots.

Until one night,

As I rubbed my belly,

I saw the truth,

And my heart became heavy.

Because there would be no double-storey home,

There would be no maple-wood cots,

No trips across the world,

And no bows speckled with pink dots.

What about school?

What about medical degree?

I stopped rubbing my stomach,

As bitterness engulfed me

I loved you,

Tracy Agidi

And you deserved so much more,

Than a mother who would regret you,

And wonder what she had you for.

I clenched the sonogram as it happened,

I imagined your blonde curls as it took place,

I whispered a list of names as it occurred,

And as I walked home, I saw your darling face.

You would be five now,

Giving me a kiss,

About to enter nursery,

But because of me you never got this.

Yet here I am,

Age 21, about to face the world,

But all I can think about,

Are those ten little fingers, and ten little toes

3(vi): Boys cry too

I can hear their laughs,

Dark and hollow,

I let the phone drop

And let the tears fall,

The sobs rack my body,

The salt sting my bruises,

I look up at the mirror,

And wonder how I got here?

And I am eighteen,

Working at the mechanics,

Rust staining my knees,

Soot covering my cheeks,

When she walked in,

And her smile was beautiful,

Her eyes like autumn leaves,

I gave a shy grin,

And she gave a bold wink back,

And I am twenty-two,

Her fingers are warm as she slides the ring on,

Her dark hair is in ringlets,

Tracy Agidi

That I press my hands into as I kiss her,

She pinches the flesh of my hand,

Leaves a dark purple bruise,

I messed up her hair a bit,

I close my eyes and wince,

And I am thirty,

As I place the baby into the cot,

And close the door so the kids can't hear,

She screams at me,

Wine glass in her hand,

I try to duck beneath the table,

As she throws it on my face,

I tell my mates I'm busy,

When they ask why I can't go to the bar,

They make jokes about the missus,

As I apply anti-septic to my scars,

She crawls beside me in the tub,

Mascara dripping down her face,

She gently kisses my cheeks and chest,

Asks me to forgive,

I do,

The manifesto on a beautiful society

Asks me to kiss her back,

I do,

Asks me to buy some cigarettes for her,

I do,

Every bruise she created,

Every scar she fashioned,

Every mark she made,

I never said a word about,

Until one day she comes home,

And the twins left their toys on the floor,

And she trips,

And she screams,

And she shouts,

And she hits and smacks and slaps and hurts and hurts and hurts and hurts and hurts

And she only stops when I grab her,

 And wrestle her to the floor,

And lock her into the bathroom,

Nine-one-one operator, what is you emergency?

My wife....wife...sh-she hit me. I'm also worried for the safety of my chil—

Wait...did you say your wife hit you?

31

Y-yes-yes officer, my wife has been abusing me for the past few years. I am also worried for---

(STATIC) *Hey – guys do you here this? This man is calling me cuz his wife is beating him up* (Laughter)

I can hear their laughs,

Dark and hollow,

I let the phone drop

And let the tears fall,

The sobs rack my body,

The salt sting my bruises,

I look up at the mirror,

And wonder how I got here?